P7-ETI-163

by John
Sazaklis

SWAMP THING
VS THE
ZOMBIE PETS

illustrated by
Art Baltazar

Swamp Thing created by
Len Wein and Bernie Wrightson

Picture Window Books™
a capstone imprint

Starring...

THE DOWN HOME CRITTER GANG!

ACE
THE BAT-HOUND!

THE UNDEAD PET CLUB!

SWAMP THING!

SOLOMON GRUNDY!

BATMAN!

TABLE OF CONTENTS!

SUPER-PET HERO FILE 022:
DOWN HOME CRITTER GANG

STARLENE
Species: Raccoon
Power: Stompin'

MOSSY
Species: Skunk
Power: Stinkin'

LOAFERS
Species: Basset Hound
Power: Snoozin'

MERLE
Species: Possum
Power: Swingin'

Super Hero Owner:
SWAMP THING

Bio: Members of the Down Home Critter Gang were born on a bayou. Like their super hero owner, Swamp Thing, they'll stop at nothing to protect their sacred swamps from Solomon Grundy's Undead Pet Club and other toxic terrors.

Super-Pet Enemy File 022:
UNDEAD PET CLUB

MAMA RIPPLES
Species: Manx Cat
Power: Howlin'

LIMPY
Species: Possum
Power: Hangin'

FAYE PRECIOUS
Species: Persian Cat
Power: Hoardin'

OFFIE LEE
Species: Hound Dog
Power: Houndin'

Super-villain Owner:
SOLOMON GRUNDY

Chapter 1

DOWN HOME CRITTERS

One muggy day, **Swamp Thing** and his **Down Home Critter Gang** enjoyed a lazy afternoon in their swamp. They spread out on a big ol' log and relaxed.

"Sure is nice, lying around doing nothing," said **Mossy** the skunk.

"And if anyone's good at doing nothing, it's **Loafers** over there," replied **Starlene** the raccoon.

A droopy-eyed basset hound lifted his head and grunted. Loafers would rather snooze than do anything else.

"Life doesn't get better than this," agreed **Merle** the possum. "Soaking up sun and breathing sweet, sweet air."

The critters took a deep breath . . . then started coughing horribly.

"What is that stench?!" cried Starlene, covering her nose.

"Sorry," said Mossy. The skunk let loose a foul odor any time he lifted his tail. And old Mossy lifted his tail quite often!

Swamp Thing jumped to his feet.

"Something terrible is happening," the eco-hero said.

"Yeah, Mossy done gone and stunk up the place again!" shouted Merle the possum. He wildly fanned the air.

"No," replied Swamp Thing. The hero leaned down. He put his hand to the ground. His special connection with the earth told him there was trouble in a nearby swamp.

Suddenly, a dark shadow fell over Swamp Thing. The hero looked up. A large object had blocked out the sun.

It was the **Batplane!** The aircraft landed, and its doors opened. **Batman** and **Ace the Bat-Hound** hopped out. They greeted Swamp Thing and the Down Home Critter Gang.

 **"What brings you so far from Gotham City?"** Swamp Thing asked the hero and his hound.

 **"We need your help,"** Batman replied. The Dark Knight explained that a fire was destroying the Great Dismal Swamp miles away. Batman wanted Swamp Thing to aid in the rescue effort.

"We should leave at once!" Swamp Thing said.

Batman nodded. He let Swamp Thing board the Batplane first.

For Swamp Thing's help, Ace agreed

to stay behind with the Down Home

Critter Gang. The Bat-Hound would

help protect their home while Swamp

Thing was away.

WOOOOOSH!

As the heroes zoomed off, Starlene approached Ace. "On behalf of the Down Home Critter Gang, we'd like to welcome you to our swamp!" she said.

 **"Thank you,"** Ace said to the raccoon. **"Nice mask, by the way."**

 **Starlene blushed.**

Ace turned to the rest of the critters. "All right, team," he said. "Who wants to take the first watch?"

"Easy there, cowboy," said Merle the possum. "Where do ya think you are?"

"Yeah, this isn't Gotham City," added Mossy the skunk. "Nothing exciting ever happens 'round here."

As the critters continued their naps, Ace took his post. He would silently guard the swamp . . . alone.

* * *

Meanwhile, the fire continued in the Great Dismal Swamp. The evil **Solomon Grundy** and his **Undead Pet Club** often haunted this area. The zombie pets included **Offie Lee** the bloodhound and **Faye Precious** the Persian cat. There was **Limpy** the possum and **Mama Ripples** the manx.

As firefighters tackled the flames, Grundy and his zombie pets fled their burial plots. They set out in search of a new place to get some eternal sleep.

"Well, this is a fine to-do!" growled

Mama Ripples. Her jowls jiggled. Her

cat eyes twitched with anger.

"How are we supposed to rest in

peace around here?" grumbled Offie

Lee, the bloodless bloodhound.

"Patience, my zombie pets," Grundy replied. "We'll find a new home. And once we do, we'll have our revenge! Those horrible humans will pay for ruining our final resting place."

"I saw a nice, muddy swamp down yonder," said Limpy the possum. He pointed with his stump. "Bet it's got all sorts of fixins for everybody!"

"Fantastic!" said Grundy. He grinned from ear to ear with a mouthful of crooked yellow teeth. **"Let's make ourselves at home."**

Chapter 2

THE UNDEAD PET CLUB

Meanwhile, Ace the Bat-Hound watched the sun set at the swamp. Suddenly, a twig snapped in the distance. Then another and another.

Ace's ears perked up. He smelled something awful, like rotten eggs.

"Get up!" Ace barked at the Down Home Critter Gang. "I smell trouble!"

Mossy, Merle, and Starlene slowly strolled over. Loafers lifted his head, grunted, and went back to sleep.

The foul smell grew more powerful. The critters glared at Mossy the skunk. "It wasn't me!" he cried.

Through the trees appeared the grimiest, creepiest creatures that Ace had ever seen. Behind them was a hulking undead brute.

 **"Solomon Grrrrrundy,"**

growled Ace. "I recognize him from his criminal file on the Batcomputer."

"And that must be his Undead Pet Club," said Merle the possum.

"Dear me!" gasped Starlene the raccoon. "I thought they were just a bunch of old ghost stories!"

"They look real to me," said Merle.

"They smell really bad, too," added Mossy the skunk, glad that he hadn't caused a stinky situation for once.

Grundy walked up to Ace. "You must be Batman's dog," he said with a snarl. "You belong in a cave, not a swamp. Go fetch a Batarang!"

HAR! HAR! HAR! The zombie pets laughed at their leader's joke. They circled the swamp. They dragged their limp limbs through the dirt.

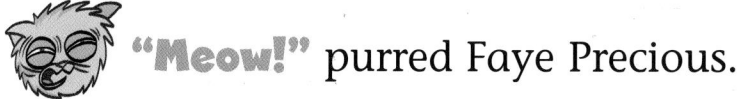 **"Meow!"** purred Faye Precious. "This soil is so moist and delicious." The filthy feline smeared dirt on her face. She licked her paws. "A girl could get used to this!"

Offie Lee started eating the dirt too. "Yup, I'm sure going to like it down here," said the bloodless bloodhound.

 **"What's this all about?"** asked Ace.

 **"We're moving in,"** said Mama Ripples. **"This here's _our_ swamp now!"**

"This is the perfect place to begin my evil plan," Grundy explained. "Under the full moon, overlooking the swamp, I will bring back hundreds of pets from beyond the grave. Every pet cemetery across the globe will unleash its zombie forces!"

"I don't think so," Ace barked back.

"Those passed-away pets are staying

put. We'll stop your evil plan!"

Mossy the skunk raised his tail. He

let loose a spray of toxic fumes.

PFFFFFFFT!

"Cute trick," said Limpy. The zombie possum and the other Undead Pets grabbed their noses. They pulled them off! "But we've got a few of our own."

Once the stench had disappeared, the zombies put their noses back on.

"Get 'em!" yelled Mama Ripples.

The zombie pets attacked the Down Home Critter Gang. Mama Ripples and Faye Precious jumped on Ace. The fat zombie cats used all their weight to hold down the heroic hound.

"Now it's your turn to play dead," hissed Faye Precious.

Offie Lee chased after Starlene and Mossy. The bloodless bloodhound left a trail of fiery slobber. Drops of spit landed on their tails, fizzling the fur.

They ran in circles until, at the last second, Starlene and Mossy scurried up a tree. Offie Lee couldn't stop in time. The pooch pounded his head against the trunk.

THWAAACK!

"I hope that knocked some sense into him," said Starlene the raccoon.

Meanwhile, the two possums faced off. Limpy tackled Merle to the ground. "I give up!" yelled Merle.

"That was too easy," grumbled Limpy. He backed off of his enemy.

"Ha! I was just playing possum!" cried Merle. "Gotcha!" He grabbed Limpy by the tail. Merle swung the zombie possum around and around.

"Surprise!" shouted Limpy. His tail snapped off, and the zombie possum flew away.

THUD! The zombie possum landed on a log . . . right next to Loafers!

The sleepy basset hound lifted up his head. He saw a delicious bone peeking out of Limpy's zombie skin.

Instantly, Loafers picked the possum up by his leg. He carried the zombie possum through the woods.

After a few paces, Loafers dug a hole and dropped Limpy into it. Before the zombie pet could do anything, Loafers buried him like a bone.

Loafers patted the pile of dirt. Then he went back to napping.

Meanwhile, the moon was about to reach its highest point in the sky. Solomon Grundy headed back to the swamp to perform his evil spell.

For the spell to work, Grundy needed to stand over the swamp. He had to look at his reflection in the water with the moon behind him. Once Grundy said the magic words, within moments all the pets that had passed away would rise from their graves.

"The Undead Pet Club is about to welcome millions of new members!" Grundy said. He cackled into the night. **"Rise, zombie pets! Rise!"**

Chapter 3

SAVING THE SWAMP

At the same time, Ace broke free from his feline foes. The Bat-Hound ran to a clearing. Mama and Faye blocked him on either side.

"Hey, cats!" yelled Ace. "Catch me if you can!"

"Come to mama!" shouted the fat cat. She leaped into the air.

With his lightning-fast reflexes, the Bat-Hound dodged the attack. Mama Ripples landed on Faye Precious.

"That's one flat cat," Ace joked.

Merle the possum scurried over with some vines from the swamp.

ZOOOMM! ZOOOMM!

The possum zipped around the zombie cats and the other Undead Pets. Soon, they were all tied up tight.

With the Undead Pet Club in a

real bind, Ace headed off to find

Solomon Grundy.

The Bat-Hound followed the

zombie's scent to a large boulder.

The villain was standing at the top,

overlooking the swamp. Grundy began

to speak the magic words.

 **"Not another word,"** said

Ace. **"It's time to play Fetch!"**

The zombie villain turned in time to

see Ace throw a Batarang.

Grundy caught the gadget with his
teeth. He bit the weapon in half.

"It's going to take more than a
simple chew toy to stop me!" he yelled.
The villain lifted the boulder over his
head. "Now it's your turn. Catch!"

Grundy threw the giant rock at the Bat-Hound. Ace flipped backward out of the way. The boulder landed in the swamp.

"Curses!" yelled Grundy. Now he'd have to wait for the water to settle to see his reflection again. "At least I have the full moon — HUH?!"

Suddenly, the moon disappeared. Grundy and Ace looked up to see a familiar shape.

The **Batplane!** It flew silently above

them, blocking the full moon.

Batman saluted Ace from the

cockpit. The bay door opened, and

Swamp Thing jumped out.

 **"More swamp trouble,"**

sighed Swamp Thing as he landed.

"Time to wrap things up."

Swamp Thing placed his hands on the ground. He used his powers to control the nearby roots and vines.

Quickly and silently, they crept up and around Grundy's body. He fought the flora, but he was overpowered.

Soon, the zombie villain was tangled in a web of vines. Grundy could not move his arms or legs.

"That's enough out of you," Swamp Thing said. Then he turned to Ace. "Thank you for your help, Bat-Hound."

Batman landed his plane. The Dark Knight relayed the news that the fire at Great Dismal Swamp was out. The ecosystem would need time to recover.

Swamp Thing turned to Solomon Grundy and said, "You and your ghoulish gang are welcome to stay at the swamp. You can become members of the Down Home Critter Gang . . . if you behave nicely."

"*Mmbbmm,*" Grundy grumbled beneath the vines.

 **"I'll take that as a Yes,"** Swamp Thing said. He released the tangled zombie.

Solomon Grundy, Batman, Ace, and Swamp Thing returned to their friends.  **"Did y'all save the day?"** Starlene asked Ace.

"The spell didn't succeed," Ace replied. He placed a paw on Starlene's shoulder. **"We saved the day together."** Starlene blushed again.

Batman and Ace bid their friends farewell. They headed back to Gotham.

Swamp Thing asked his pets to untie the Undead Pet Club. "They are going to stay with us for a while," he said.

"That isn't so bad," Merle said. "This is one zombie attack I can handle."

All of a sudden, a loud moan pierced the silence. Then a scratching sound was heard from the forest. The Down Home Critters started shivering. They saw a pile of dirt moving nearby.

A clawed paw peeked out from the soil, followed by a rotten limb. Something was rising from a grave!

"I thought you said the spell didn't work!" Starlene shouted at Mossy.

"More zombies?!" gasped Merle.

The creature limped toward the group. It shook off the dirt and stepped into the moonlight.

"Limpy!" cheered the Undead Pets. The zombie possum had fallen asleep where Loafers had buried him.

"Ah, nothing lets you rest in peace like a good dirt nap," Limpy said.

Loafers lifted his head and agreed. The Down Home Critter Gang and the Undead Pet Club were going to get along just fine. **END!**

KNOW YOUR HERO PETS!

KNOW YOUR VILLAIN PETS!

1. Bizarro Krypto
2. Ignatius
3. Brainicat
4. Mechanikat
5. Dogwood
6. General Manx
7. Nizz
8. Fer-El
9. Crackers
10. Giggles
11. Artie Puffin
12. Griff
13. Waddles
14. Rozz
15. Mad Catter
16. Croward
17. Chauncey
18. Bit-Bit & X-43
19. Dr. Spider
20. Anna Conda
21. Mr. Mind
22. Sobek
23. Patches
24. Dex-Starr
25. Glomulus
26. Titano
27. Purring Pete
28. Kid Kitty
29. Scratchy Tom
30. Gat-Cat
31. Starro
32. Mama Ripples
33. Faye Precious
34. Limpy
35. Offie Lee
36. Misty
37. Sneezers
38. Johnny
39. Joey
40. Frankie
41. George
42. Whoosh
43. Pronto
44. Snorrt
45. Rolf
46. Squealer
47. Kajunn
48. Tootz
49. Eezix
50. Donald
51. Waxxee
52. Fimble
53. Webbik

MEET THE AUTHOR!

John Sazaklis

John Sazaklis, a *New York Times* bestselling author, enjoys writing children's books about his favorite characters. To him, it's a dream come true. He has been reading comics and watching cartoons since before even the Internet! John lives with his beautiful wife in the Big Apple.

MEET THE ILLUSTRATOR!

Eisner Award-winner Art Baltazar

Art Baltazar is a cartoonist machine from the heart of Chicago! He defines cartoons and comics not only as an art style, but as a way of life. Currently, Art is the creative force behind *The New York Times* best-selling, Eisner Award-winning, DC Comics series Tiny Titans, and the co-writer for *Billy Batson and the Magic of SHAZAM!* Art is living the dream! He draws comics and never has to leave the house. He lives with his lovely wife, Rose, big boy Sonny, little boy Gordon, and little girl Audrey. Right on!

WORD POWER!

brute (BROOT)—a nonhuman creature or beast

dismal (DIZ-muhl)—gloomy and sad

ecosystem (EE-koh-siss-tuhm)—a community of animals and plants interacting with their environment

flora (FLOR-uh)—the plant life in a particular area

jowl (JOUL)—a layer of loose flesh that hangs down around the throat or lower jaw

muggy (MUH-gee)—warm and damp weather

reflection (ri-FLEKT-shuhn)—the reproduction of an image on a shiny surface, such as a mirror

toxic (TOK-sik)—poisonous, or dangerous to digest

zombie (ZAHM-bee)—a person who is believed to have died and been brought back to life

HERO DOGS
GALORE!

SPACE CANINE
PATROL AGENCY!

KRYPTO THE
SUPER-DOG!

BATCOW!

FLUFFY AND THE
AQUA-PETS!

PLASTIC
FROG!

JUMPA
THE KANGA!

STORM AND THE
AQUA-PETS!

STREAKY
THE SUPER-CAT!

THE TERRIFIC
WHATZIT!

SUPER-TURTLE!

BIG TED
AND DAWG!

Read all of these totally awesome stories today, starring all of your favorite DC SUPER-PETS!

GREEN LANTERN BUG CORPS!

SPOT!

ROBIN ROBIN AND ACE TEAM-UP!

SPACE CANINE PATROL AGENCY!

HOPPY!

BEPPO THE SUPER-MONKEY!

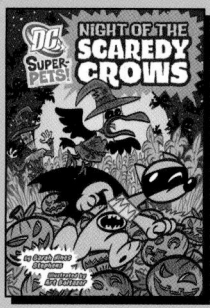
ACE THE BAT-HOUND!

KRYPTO AND ACE TEAM-UP!

B'DG, THE GREEN LANTERN!

THE LEGION OF SUPER-PETS!

COMET THE SUPER-HORSE!

DOWN HOME CRITTER GANG!

Picture Window Books™

Published in 2012
A Capstone Imprint
1710 Roe Crest Drive
North Mankato, MN 56003
www.capstonepub.com

STAR26101

Cataloging-in-Publication Data is available at the Library of Congress website.
ISBN: 978-1-4048-6491-7 (library binding)
ISBN: 978-1-4048-7667-5 (paperback)

Summary: While Swamp Thing stomps out a local forest fire, the eco-hero's bog buddies face an even greater threat...Solomon Grundy! This fiend and his Undead Pet Club are planning to revive all the dead pets in the world — and then take it over! If the Down Home Critters can't stop their evil plot, they'll all be in grave danger.

Art Director & Designer: Bob Lentz
Editor: Donald Lemke
Creative Director: Heather Kindseth
Editorial Director: Michael Dahl

Printed in the United States of America in Stevens Point, Wisconsin.
032012   006678WZF12